MW00876221

Hey Silly Milly!

By Milan Hoy

Written by Milan Hoy
Illustrated by Anastacia Kosata
Edited by Lakeshia Hoy
ISBN: 9781734282702

There once lived a girl who was really silly.
She was 6 years old, and her name was Milly.

She loved to draw, sing, and dance,
but she only wore polka dot pants.

Milly and her siblings loved to play.
They jumped, ran, and hid all day.

"Milly! Milly! Where are you?"
She jumped from behind the tree and yelled, "Peek-a-boo!"

She rolled down hills and picked pretty flowers.
She made funny faces in the mirror for hours!

One day, on her way to school.
Milly had an idea she thought was cool.

She collected a big jar of ants to train,
then taught the ants to spell her name.

Milly brought the ants for show and tell.
Finn bumped the jar, and all the ants fell.

She laughed and couldn't help but giggle,
as she watched her friends jump and wiggle.

Her teacher jumped in surprise to see such a display.
Milly laughed so hard that she decided to play.

She dropped some ants on her pants too.
The whole class laughed until their faces turned blue.

"Silly Milly!" said Ms.Hershey, "We need a plan."

Milly suggested, "How about an ant marching band?"

"Great idea Milly, but how about something sweet?
We can give the ants sugar cubes to eat!"

The teacher told the kids, "Time to follow me!"
Then she dropped sugar cubes leading to a tree.

"Now jump, shake, wiggle, dance...
till all the ants are off your pants!"

Ms. Hershey said, "Okay kids, time for a snack!
The food is in class, so let's go back."

Robert said, "Can we eat our snack out here?
It's nice and bright, and the weather is clear!"

When the teacher agreed, they returned to class.
They grabbed their snacks and a blanket for the grass.

When all was set, they began to eat.
Milly thought, maybe the ants want another treat.

She dropped some of her food near the tree.
She told the ants, "Hey, come with me!"

The students were laughing and enjoying their snacks.
They dropped food crumbs all over their laps.

Pretty soon, the kids began to wiggle and dance.
The ants once again began to crawl on their pants.

"Oops! Silly Milly!"

Made in the USA
Columbia, SC
08 September 2021